Time Traveller

Sarah Lacey

Time Traveller

Sarah Lacey

Elizabeth Dye

Illustrated by Geraldine Mitchell

Seven Arches Publishing

Published in June 2011
By Seven Arches Publishing
27, Church Street, Nassington, Peterborough PE8 61QG
www.sevenarchespublishing.co.uk

A catalogue record for this book is available from the British Library.

Cover design, scans and typesetting by Alan McGlynn.

Printed in Great Britain by imprintdigital.net

ISBN 978-0-9567572-1-0

To all the children in Derbyshire primary schools

Elizabeth Dye was born and brought up in rural Essex. It was when she started teaching in a primary school in Derby that she came to realise the unbearably harsh conditions for children working in mines and mills in the nineteenth century in the north of England. The story of the disaster at Huskar Colliery near the village of Silkstone is what inspired the writing of this book, along with the happenings at Magpie mine in Derbyshire. The names of the children who died in the disaster are recorded in Silkstone parish church and their deaths are commemorated on the Huskar memorial just outside the village.

‹IF THIS IS THE FIRST TIME YOU HAVE READ ONE OF THE BOOKS THAT RECORDS THE ADVENTURES OF CHILDREN FROM THE TWENTY FIRST CENTURY IN A TIMEZONE DIFFERENT TO TODAY. YOU NEED TO KNOW›

› That SHARP stands for The Scientific History and Art Reclamation Programme.

› That STRAP stands for the Scientific Testing and Recording of Aggression Programme.

› That time slip is something that you might suffer if you travel through time and space, in a similar way to how some people get jet lag when they fly long distances on a jet air liner.

› That if you travel through time and space you are a xrosmonaut.

CHAPTER 1

Water Phobia

<u>12 Boundary Road.</u>

'Run, Sarah, run! Come on. Get up! Run!'

The boy grabbed her arm and tugged her up onto her feet. He stumbled forward, trying to drag her behind him. But she couldn't follow: she didn't seem to be able to move.

Why must she run?

The boy turned. His face, screwed tight with fear and streaked black with grime, came close to hers.

'Do you want to drown or summat?' he yelled.

Drown? Of course not! Her feet seemed to come free, and suddenly she was running after this strange boy down the twisting, dark tunnel; running as fast as she could, her lungs gasping for air.

Now there were many more than the two of them; children running in front of her, behind her on both sides, all shouting: 'Drown....drown!' Other sounds as well. Behind her she could hear the roaring, sloshing sound of torrents of water coming ever nearer.

'Drown!' the words filled her ears.

'Drown!' Now she too was shouting.

The boy and the other children were going faster than she was, getting further away down the tunnel; there seemed to be something tripping her up, catching at her feet.

Somebody (or was it something?) held her down, stopping her from running. She lashed out at whatever it was. She was not going to stay and drown.

Then she heard another voice saying:

'Sarah! Sarah, please stop thumping me. It's all right, my darling. You're safe; just calm down.' That was her mum's voice. Sarah realised, with a sudden confused shock, that the boy and the dark tunnel had disappeared. But she was still unable to move freely. She was trapped. She tried to kick and to stretch out her arms but it was impossible.

'Hang on, you've got yourself all wrapped up in your sheet. Sarah, lie still and I'll unwrap you.'

And it was then that she felt the warmth of her own bed, her mum's breath on her cheek, her mum's arms moving around her. She could see the outlines of the curtains, the blur of her mum's short blonde hair.

'Horrid, horrid nightmare, my love. You were bellowing at the top of your voice; woke the whole house up.'

Slowly Sarah sat up and took in her mother's anxious face. Looking down, she saw that her bed was a confused and twisted mass of covers. She was hot, wet with sweat, and her heart was thumping in her chest.

'Nightmare?' she asked slowly.

'You were yelling, 'Run, run, drown, drown!' said her mum. 'I couldn't wake you up, and when I tried to, you bashed me in the face.'

'Sorry, I thought we were all going to drown. So I had to run away.'

Her mum sat on the edge of the now straightened bedclothes and stroked Sarah's hair, short and blonde like her own.

'It's those special lessons, isn't it? The extra swimming lessons. You've had an anxiety dream – no, an anxiety nightmare.'

Sarah wanted to block out the nightmare from her thoughts. She was not going to let the dark, the wet, the sound of rushing water get a finger-hold on her mind. But the reality of the swimming lessons…now that was something she had to think about. Tomorrow, well, no, more than likely today she was having extra special, very generously donated, and much feared swimming lessons.

If there was one thing in the whole world that Sarah hated, it was water: cold, deep, squashy water. Ever since she had been a tiny child, when she would scream the house down every time she had had her hair washed, she had hated water: water in her ears; water on her eyes; water up her nose. She could just about lower herself into a bath, because she could see the bottom of a bath and she could hold onto the sides. But there was no way she would get under a shower. She was not going to willingly allow all that water into her ears, mouth, or nose. She was not going down the slide at the swimming pool. She was not going to laugh and jump when a wave bashed into her legs, but instead would stand petrified on the edge of the great, rocking, rolling sea. Water dragged you down, bowled you over and poured down your throat.

She was such a clever, sensible girl in all other ways, and talented and imaginative.

'Too much imagination,' her grandmother had once snapped crossly, although she loved Sarah and was delighted that Sarah had rung up on her birthday.

'Which year were you actually born, Gran?' she had asked.

'1940. One year after the Second World War

started.'

'That's funny – we're doing what happened round about 1840 in history at school. All about children in factories and things. Think, if you'd been born just one hundred years earlier you could've been up a chimney, or down a mine, or working sixteen hours a day in a factory.'

'Well, I wasn't. And 1940 was bad enough, I can tell you. No nice things like swimming lessons,' said her gran, still blonde and smart, like her mother.

Her mother had called it: 'water phobia.' She had explained to the teachers at school: 'Sarah suffers from water phobia.' The teachers had nodded and smiled, but looked unconvinced, and Sarah still went to swimming lessons in Years 5 and 6.

Last week, in school assembly, the real nightmare had started.

She had filed into assembly as usual, and sat comfortably next to her best friend, Agna. She had expected to spend the next twenty minutes as usual, pleasantly daydreaming while the teachers did their best to get 250 children excited about being kind and thoughtful to each other, or possibly to some more unfortunate child in another part of the world.

But that day, there on the stage in front of the

whole school, had been some bigwig from the leisure services, trumpeting on about how every child in the borough (what in heaven's name was that? She thought a borough was where a whole lot of rabbits lived, but he certainly wasn't talking about rabbits) – yes, every child in the borough had the fantastic opportunity to learn how to swim.

Then he gave out all the swimming awards for her class, Year 6. Five children went up to get their 500 metres award, fifteen had their 200 metres, six with 100 metres, and three little strugglers with only 20 metres. There was a great deal of clapping, there were lots of smiles and all those with awards had little metal medals on ribbons.

And then right at the end, he had said:

'And to show how committed we of the Leisure Services are to ensure that every child in the borough can swim, we are PROUD to announce here today that for the very first time we have initiated the only scheme in the entire country where children who cannot swim at all… (long, long pause) … children who are at serious risk to life and limb are being presented with the chance to participate in our 'Swim for Your Life' scheme'.'

He flapped a gold-edged booklet, and picked up

a pair of gold-rimmed goggles and a sort of duffle bag decorated with a huge, gold-coloured whale, which was clever enough to be able to laugh and blow bubbles at the same time. All the smaller children 'oohed' and 'aahed' – perhaps they would get a bag with a gold whale – and all the children who could swim pulled sharp faces.

'So, Sarah Lacey, you have been chosen to take part in the first batch of would-be swimmers.' And he fluttered the booklet towards her, and to her horror Sarah found herself being shoved forward towards the stage to accept the one offer she had no desire whatsoever to receive: six concentrated swimming lessons on Saturday morning with a unknown bunch of no-hopers like herself, ominously called, 'Swim for Your Life.'

Sarah could feel her face going redder and redder. She could see the smug swimmers in her class smirking and she wanted to shout: 'I don't want to be able to swim. I HATE WATER!' Finally, as the last nail in her coffin, she heard the man say:

'And guess what, children? We expect to get the TV blokes to cover the event. How about that, Sarah?'

CHAPTER 2

Six Fingers, One Thumb

'But…' (Agna nearly always started her sentences with either 'but' or 'and') '…remember when we went to Alton Towers you tried every one of the rides except the log flume, and I didn't go on a single ride.'

'Yes?'

'And, when your mother had a chip-pan fire, you saved her life by throwing tea towels over the fire, even though the flames were reaching the ceiling.'

'Yes? So what?'

'And…so, it's not that you're a wimp who is scared of everything; you can cope with heights and with fire – it's just water that gets to you (and rats, of course),' Agna concluded.

'I suppose so, but they didn't need to get me up there in front of the whole school like that, did they?' Sarah kicked the toes of her shoes against anything that presented itself to her.

'And…that was victimisation. It was not PC; it was discrimination against people with water-phobia and should not have been allowed.' Agna was in her stride now and Sarah smiled. She wished that Agna was a non-swimmer: then they could have gone to the classes together.

Now, though, it was Saturday morning and Sarah was in a taxi with five other non-swimmers being whisked across to Moorlands Pool on the other side of town. In her family, Saturday mornings were special: her lovely ditzy-glitzy mother went shopping, her quiet sensible father went to the allotment, and she went to the museum. Every Saturday at the museum there was an interactive science session. Last week they had made slime balls. This week they were going to make plastic foam. Ordinarily afterwards, she, mum and dad would have met up for coffee and doughnuts in the museum cafe. But instead she was on her way to Moorlands Pool. The only thing she knew about Moorlands was that it had an Olympic-sized pool where all the Olympic hopefuls practised at six o'clock every morning.

They all sat in dejected silence; six children united by an inability to swim. Sarah's phone buzzed. She felt a moment of hope that somehow it was going to be a message telling her the whole thing was being called off.

'X channel swim nxt yr?'

It was a message from Agna. Sarah put the phone down on the seat next to her and started to count cars.

'I was supposed to be going to the museum,' muttered the small, dark boy sitting next to her.

'So was I,' said Sarah.

Like a prisoner facing the firing squad, she felt a sort of miserable companionship with the other children. It confirmed what she had always believed: children had no rights. They had to do what their parents, their teachers, the government, everybody told them to do. Why, even the dinner ladies could stop you if you chose chips too many times in one week. Adults said they were listening to you, but they weren't.

'This is our Olympic-sized pool,' declared the swimming-pool lady proudly as she shepherded her little gang of visibly shrinking non-swimmers through the pool complex. 'Of course, you will not be here. Before the rest of the public arrive we have allocated you the 'Wet Tummy Roll Around'.'

Sweeping through some swing doors, she ushered them purposefully into an area obviously designed for the under-fives.

It was a rounded pool, very shallow, perhaps just

ten centimetres deep at the edges, and full of little colourful mushroom-shaped islands with narrow channels in between. Here and there small jets of water bubbled up and then subsided, only to bubble up again a few minutes later. It was not in the least scary and there was nobody else in the place, except… Bill.

'Hi folks! I'm Bill!' A short man in a sporty track-suit bounced towards them. 'They chose me to get you all afloat because…' at that point he whispered something. All the children leaned forward, Sarah included.

'What did you say?' asked the skinny girl with legs purple with cold, or perhaps fear.

'… because,' still in a whisper, 'I hate water!' At which point he roared with laughter. 'All those other teachers tell you to learn to love the water. NO folks! Don't do that, because water is not going to love you! But be just one bit cleverer than that it is. Be one step ahead! It might be cold and wet and deep and determined to get into your ears, but you are the ones who are bright enough to outwit it at every turn.'

Sarah stared at this Bill person. He was a round, smiley man. He moved his hands a lot when he spoke, almost as if he thought they were deaf and needed hand signals to understand. Sarah decided that she liked him. And what is more, the 'Wet Tummy Roll

Around' pool looked fun.

When they had all changed into their swimming things, Bill put them into pairs. Sarah was paired up with the boy called Anniz. He was quiet and dark-skinned with strange eyes that seemed to change colour from light toffee to deep, glossy chestnut every time she looked at them. He was the one who thought he was going to the museum and had ended up at the pool. Perhaps his parents had lied to him, just to get him to go.

The lesson, if that was what it was, consisted of a lot of splashing, a lot of crawling, and a lot of rolling and nosing big red balls through the narrow channels and round the little islands. She and Anniz laughed and chased each other with more excited enthusiasm than any of the others in the group. Finally, lying there in the warm water just a few centimetres deep and feeling it almost lift up their arms and legs with a gentle rocking, they had all got their hair wet, their ears and eyes wet, and nobody had panicked.

Then Bill took them through to the big pool and asked them to sit on the edge with their feet dangling into the clear blue depths. Sarah was on the end of the line, the farthest away from Bill, sitting next to Anniz. Bill outlined what they were going to do the following week. She tried hard to listen to him telling them that next week they would walk across the pool at the shallow end, but his words drifted off across the vast expanse of Olympic pool and she found herself looking down at Anniz's hand. There was something very odd about it. She counted his fingers. He had six fingers, not four – seven digits in all. The hand on the side of the pool next to her had six fingers! What did that mean? Was it a deformity? She'd never known such a thing!

Anniz turned his head away from Bill and looked at Sarah. He winked. Then he turned back and seemed to listen intently to what Bill was saying.

'Well, folks, that's it for this week. You've all been fantastic! Who's looking forward to coming back next week?' Hands shot up in the air, including Anniz's. It was the hand on the other side to Sarah. Sarah's hand didn't go up with the others because she was busy trying to count the fingers on the one Anniz had raised, but it was shut in a fist.

'Sarah?' said Bill looking down the line at her. 'You don't seem too sure. Didn't you like the session?'

'Oh yes, Bill, it was great – I was just thinking how hungry I felt.'

At that, some of the others giggled and one child

said: 'Me too.'

'Well,' Bill went on, 'after you've all got changed, we've got a treat for you all, for doing so well today. There are drinks and snacks on offer – really good ones.'

As they trouped back to the changing rooms, shivering a little now, Sarah was about to ask Anniz about his hand and to find out if he had as many fingers on the other one, but she didn't because it seemed rude. He turned round to Sarah to say:

'Bet I'm changed and ready before you.'

'Bet you're not,' said Sarah, grabbing her clothes from her locker and bolting into the changing cubicle.

After a frantic rubbing down with the towel, and with her hair still damp and the collar of her top twisted under on one side, Sarah stepped out of her cubicle at the exact same time as Anniz and well before any of the others.

They laughed and ran down the corridor to the reception area. When they got there, even the adults hadn't arrived. Sarah decided that Anniz was almost a friend.

'Wow,' said Sarah, 'chocolate biscuits, crisps and Coca Cola. What are you having?'

Anniz just shook his head and fished a strange-looking bar out of this bag. Sitting down opposite him she could clearly see that his other hand had six fingers as well. Nothing else about his hands looked deformed.

'Sarah, you can ask me about it if you like,' Anniz said, as if he had read her thoughts.

'There's something odd about you, not just your hands, although that is extremely strange.'

'Of course it is.'

'Were you born with seven digits?'

'No, we have them grafted on not long after birth; that is, if families can afford it. It's useful and a kind of fashion statement as well.'

'What? It's fashionable to have extra fingers? I don't think so! Does your granny knit gloves for you all? Nobody round here thinks extra fingers are cool!'

'That's it, Sarah,' he took a quick bite from his snack and Sarah watched in amazement as it slowly regained it's original size, 'I don't really come from round here.'

Now he was leaning forward and speaking quickly, and so quietly that he was almost whispering, 'I'm from the future – same world but a future one.' As Anniz spoke he looked at Sarah very intently. She found that she couldn't look away. She tried to, but it was as if she were being hypnotised. He was scaring her now – was he teasing her, or did he really believe this stuff he was coming out with?

He put one hand on the table in front of her and turned the palm upwards. There were numbers tattooed across it: **10812**. He rubbed his hands together and then showed her the inside of his hand again. The numbers had gone.

'What number did you see on the palm of my hand?' Anniz asked.

'10812,' Sarah answered without hesitation.

He nodded.

'You see! You're exactly right to be a time traveller. You have been chosen by the organisation I work for. It's called STRAP. You need to know more about them, but I don't have the time to tell you right now. We were supposed to meet at the museum, not here at the swimming pool. All that water stuff took up much too much time.'

'I don't understand a word of what you are saying,' said Sarah, shaking her head, which seemed to free her from being held by his eyes.

Anniz dug a hand into his pocket and took out what looked like an iphone. He tapped the screen and showed her the text:

Sarah Lacey – ideal candidate for **Strap 10812** because of her capacity to observe small details and her remarkable level of courage.

'Well, what do you think?'

'I think you talk in riddles,' she replied slowly and then added, very much more quickly, 'and I think that looks like the TV crew out there.'

'Oh no!' Anniz almost squealed. 'No place for me.' He had jumped to his feet, grabbed her hand and whispered, 'Run, Sarah run!'

CHAPTER 3

Sarah Lacey TV Star

'Run!'

For a moment Sarah felt a rush of fear. That was the word the boy had screamed at her in her nightmare last night! But now all she was doing was running out of a swimming pool reception area into a large, bright sports hall set up with four table-tennis tables.

'Phew. I would have been bounced back to starter level if I'd let that happen,' Anniz declared, sinking down onto his heels, his back against the wall, his six-fingered hands splayed out across the dusty floor.

'Does your phone take pictures?' he continued. Sarah nodded; still not at all sure why she had willingly followed Anniz after he had set off on his mad flight from the TV crew.

'Take a picture of me now – and quickly because I've not got much time left. '

Totally bemused, Sarah held up her phone, focused on Anniz, pressed the photo button and gasped. There on her phone was a picture of the wall, the floor and a bit of the window, but no boy.

Nothing.

She took a second, being very careful to get him bang in the middle of the shot. Still no Anniz. Just wall and floor.

'So that poor old camera crew would have been in a fine flip-flap if they'd tried to film me. I'm unreceptive to the microdot systems used by your cameras. Oh heavens, I've only about 182 seconds left: please, please just listen. We, I mean you and me, we were supposed to meet up in the museum, and it took volcanic amounts of megabytes to get the venue changed. But when I de-energise in a few minutes time, will you please press 10812 into your phone and then that new black button; the one that wasn't there when you left your phone next to me in the taxi? I will be able to explain everything to you, but if I tell you I'm a time traveller and…' he paused.

'And if I told you I was an *X-Factor* judge,' Sarah laughed.

Anniz glanced down at his iphone-like gadget and read: 'X – unknown quantity; factor – to be considered; judge – to make a decision in a court of law?'

Sarah shook her head and rolled her eyes. 'Just tell me the story,' she sighed.

'Well, I'm just a boy who's been given a job to do.

(37 seconds before I dematerialise) and I've not done it very well so far, and if you refuse I'll be right back to base line, so please, please can you say yes?'

'Yes to what?' Sarah asked, faintly fascinated in spite of herself.

'Will you go back in time for us? It's really important.' He was obviously pleading; he had one hand held out towards her; it seemed to mean a great deal to him.

'Don't be silly…' She paused, but there before her eyes he was thinning out; he didn't look quite like a real human being any more. It was almost as if he were becoming transparent or dissolving, but still he reached towards her, begging. And not really thinking she said, 'Oh go on then. Yes.' and she saw a quick grin crease up his face, now all misty and fuzzy around the edges, as what was left of his entire shape slowly and gently evaporated into thin air.

'Sarah!'

Sarah jumped and spun round.

'Whatever are you doing in here? Come and talk to the film crew about your experience this morning.' The organising woman who had marched them past the Olympic pool was shouting to her from the doorway across the hall, and seconds later she found herself shepherded with the other four children into a tight, smiling group.

'Where is that other boy, the one we squeezed in at the last moment, that Anniz some-thing-or-other?' the woman spun round wildly.

'I think he had to go off to another appointment,' Sarah found herself saying, tempted to add 'back into outer space, I shouldn't wonder.' Considering that she had spent such a short amount of time with Anniz, she couldn't understand why she now felt so superior to everyone else. She felt as if she had been elevated to the status of a Time Lord. Here she was, a failed swimmer, exposed as a stupid child unable to manage three metres with her feet off the bottom of the pool, and yet she felt ready to take on all this noisy bunch of silly adults.

And so, that evening, after the main evening news had been broadcast, and when local events had an airing on the telly, there she was, smiling straight at the camera and saying:

'We all had a fab time. I think our local leisure services are doing a great job to make sure that every child in the borough' (she had discovered what the word borough meant) 'will be able to swim by the end of the year.' The film cut off at that point, even though she had gone on about life and limb and how next year she was planning to tackle the English Channel. Her mother was immensely proud, although Sarah now found her whole performance truly embarrassing.

'Sarah, that was just amazing you were so confident, so articulate, so grown up. I'll just pop round to see if Muriel watched it. Why don't you exercise Gonk for a bit?'

'Great, I'd love that.'

As she scooped Gonk out of his hutch, the grey, smouldering light of late evening was fading the edges of the garden. The exercise word was a slight exaggeration, as Gonk was the most timid, and possibly the most stupid, rabbit in existence. When released and placed in the centre of the lawn he would attempt a tiny hop forward, a few explorative nibbles, a lot of nose-twitching and some seriously quiet sitting.

Sarah put Gonk down at her feet and sat down on the garden bench. The Lacey garden outshone all others in the area, with shrubs, flowers and vegetables in profusion. Her dad was gardening mad. The bench where Sarah was sitting was shielded from view by a huge lilac bush. Sarah slowly took out her phone. She clicked on the photo replay and studied the two pictures she'd taken in the sports hall. He had been there, right in front of her. It was impossible to have focused on the wrong spot. But there was absolutely no sign of anyone in the photo. There was the sports hall wall with a few pegs, then the floor, nothing else. Wait. She peered carefully; she could even see the dust on the floor, and there, so faint anyone would miss it if they weren't looking for it, was a handprint.

The print of a splayed hand with the palm, a thumb and six fingers was faintly outlined in the dust. Sarah grinned, she might be unable to swim but she could follow clues with the very best of them.

He had said: 'Tap in 10812 and then press the black button.' She stared down at the phone. Across the top were three new buttons, black, red and green – buttons that had NOT been there that morning. Perhaps she could just see what happened if she pressed the green and the red. Her fingers hovered… No! No! You don't mess with time travel. He had said quite specifically: 'Tap in 10812 then press the black button.'

'One! Two! Three! Ready,' she whispered, biting her lip so hard it hurt. She tapped out the numbers 10812, took a deep breath, crossed the fingers of one hand and pressed down the black key.

CHAPTER 4

Rogue Outfit

24 Springbank Drive

A few miles away from Sarah's home, Danny Higgins, who was quite a bit older than Sarah, was staring at his computer screen in disbelief.

Things were getting pretty serious; here was another message coming in concerning STRAP. Danny had only just got back the day before from a time travel mission, having gone back to the fourteenth century to rescue a boy stranded there by these STRAP people. He was still suffering from the horrible side effects of the trip, a sort of giddy sickness. It was *time-slip*, and he always got it really badly. That was why he had been lurking all day in his bedroom, trying to shake it off so as not to let his parents or sister, Jenny, know that he was not feeling well. Now that he was a seasoned time traveller he had to cover up so much.

Danny knew that when he agreed to time travel into the past with SHARP, he was risking his life, but at least he had sound evidence that the SHARP people were to be trusted. STRAP was completely different: it was a rogue outfit, ready to sacrifice the lives of children in the twenty-first century to suit its own ends. The message on his computer screen said:

> A ten-year-old girl from your area is to be sent back to the nineteenth century by STRAP without proper precautions. **Stand by**.

He tried to read what came next, but it was no good, the words on the screen seemed to dance in front of his eyes. He would have to wait until he could settle this time-slip down.

He stood up, wandered over to the window and stared out at the row of ordinary semis on the opposite side of his street. Staring at familiar objects was one way to stop the dizziness. Not everyone who time travelled suffered with it, apparently, but Danny did. He always got it; it made him feel as if he was going to yuk up at any moment.

As he stared down at the street, he spotted the Bottomley's cat. He liked the cat, but nothing much else about the Bottomleys. It stalked down the pavement, through the gate and into the front of the Bottomley's house. Jumping up, it settled itself on the empty birdbath that was surrounded by a conglomeration of gnomes and various garden knick-knacks. Danny was sure that the Bottomleys had acquired another gnome – surely that odd shape bowling a cricket ball to the one with the bat had not been there last time he looked? After a count and a re-count, reaching 32, he knew he was right; another gnome had been added, the tally last time had been 31. The sight of the Bottomley's garden was almost painful to a boy whose bedroom was state-of-the-art unclutteredness. This time though, his grim fascination with the Bottomley's gnomes paid off and he started to feel less giddy.

He went back to the computer. The follow-on message read.

> Hi Danny. It's Kaz here. We have detected a lot of STRAP activity in your area. At first we thought they might be trying to get at you, but we got a very clear message today that their target was a ten-year-old girl called Sarah. We didn't get the rest of her name, though it might have begun with 'L.' We don't understand at all what they have been up to, but do you have organisations called 'leisure services'?

Danny sat back down in front of the computer and typed:

Yes, we do. Leisure services look after things like public libraries, sports facilities and swimming pools.

That's good to know because in some way this girl is involved with these 'leisure services.' How do you think that would be?

Well, she might be involved through some kind of a project at the library, maybe, or perhaps she's a star swimmer or something.

I am sure that info will come in useful. How are you feeling, by the way?

The time slip has been really bad – the worst I've ever had.

We knew that would happen because of the rush we had sending you off and getting you back so quickly. But you know how grateful we are that you went. That boy would have been lost forever stranded in the past, and the longer you leave someone in a time period they do not belong to, the harder it is to get them back.

Oh, I know. Of course, I was glad to help Alex – to be stranded in medieval times would be no joke. Like being dead or something. I'm going to try and contact him on facebook, by the way. I'd always be glad to help, you know, if it were needed for this Sarah whoever she is. Just contact me. Isn't ten rather young for time travel?

It's much too young, that's how despicable they are. Even the physiology isn't right; it could mess up her bone growth in the future, especially if they send her underground. Contact you soon if we hear any more. Kaz

Danny stood up and sat down again sharply as dizziness flooded his brain . Better do another gnome count, he thought. His count had got to twenty when his younger sister, Jenny, called up the stairs:

'Tea's ready, Danny.'

'I'll be down in a sec,' he shouted back down.

When he got down he found the three of them – his mum, dad and sister – sitting watching the television, quite an unusual activity in the Higgins house. The reason for it was that some local man had dug up a Viking helmet or something of the sort in his back garden, and the local news was going to cover it. With both his mum and dad being avid historians, there was no way they were going to miss this.

'I thought you said it was tea-time,' said Danny.

'Shush, sit down and don't be impatient – we haven't seen you all day,' said his mum illogically.

The item hadn't come on yet, and so they were having to wait through a post-office robbery, a report on an award-winning local restaurant, a scandal at a care home, and then something that made Danny sit up as if he'd been jabbed with a pin.

A girl about ten years old, with short blonde hair and a sunny smile, was saying to the camera:

'We all had a fab time. I think our local leisure services are doing a great job to make sure that every child in the borough will be able to swim by the end of the year.'

And the interviewer asked:

'Was that the view of all the children who attended the 'Swim for your Life' course, Sarah?'

'Oh yes, it was,' smiled the girl.

'Well, thank you, Sarah Lacey, for answering our questions, and we wish you, and all the others, the very best with the rest of your time on the swimming course.'

The next item was the one with the Viking helmet. As soon as it finished, Danny's mum switched the television off and they all went over to the table to eat. Mr and Mrs Higgins didn't hold with television-watching while tea was being eaten.

CHAPTER 5

Robin Hood Would be Good

<u>12 Boundary Road</u>

As soon as Sarah pressed the new black key on her mobile, the phone started to vibrate so violently she nearly dropped it, and then, to her utter amazement, the screen slowly and majestically expanded and appeared to float up, as though it had its own independent life force. To begin with it was a swirling blue colour, but slowly text began to come into focus.

Hello, Sarah, this is Anniz, I had such a great time today. I hope you did too. They've said it wasn't my fault that I didn't have time to explain things to you properly. As you know, we were supposed to be meeting at the museum – coming to the pool was just way out of our expectations. Anyway, I was meant to have given you a lot of information before I left you. I should have told you, that... this next bit will sound very odd to you... I, my family and all my mates and so on, we are living in your future.

He stopped for a minute and Sarah waited for the next words to come up.

Or I could say, you are living in my past. When the great collapse of society took place and the Dark Chaos followed, we lost all records of what had happened in the past. Humanity survived because there were a few individuals who were very, very scientifically and technologically advanced. Now we, that is, the survivors of humanity (who are as one: there are no separate nations), are trying to come back to discover what happened. However, we can only go back in time as far as the twenty-first century, and we cannot stay for long. I am a working student of a university organisation called STRAP, which stands for Scientific Testing and Recording of Aggression Processes – really odd name I know. It comes from the time when they were trying to discover why there were so many wars and things. I think they should have called it **WWTUBT?** What Were They Up to Back Then?'

Anniz a working student at a university? Never! Perhaps in the future you learn much quicker, Sarah thought. To her he had looked about nine years old.

My job today was to ask you, on behalf of the organisation, if you would travel back in time for STRAP, and you gave me the answer, 'yes'. Anniz

'Wait a minute, though,' Sarah said to the floating screen. 'You didn't give me any time to think about it. It's a really big thing you are asking.'

There was no acknowledgement from Anniz to this, and seconds later the following words appeared. Sarah could tell they were from some higher source – the language seemed official, grown-up and serious.

‹WELCOME, SARAH LACEY, TO STRAP 10812›

This is an invitation to join our project. We believe that you are particularly suited to this work, which should, under normal circumstance, be perfectly safe (although we cannot guarantee that certain unexpected happenings might occur). When you have read this text please think carefully about your response.

Before she could begin to think carefully, more words flashed onto the screen.

What you do with us as a time traveller will be of immense help to the whole of the future human race.

Well, of course she would want to help with that.

If you agree, we will provide you with a small time/space travel bag containing a silver coloured disc. The bag attaches itself to you without any straps or adhesives. Both the bag and the disc are vital for the success of you mission.

The screen changed once more and now there were flashing numbers, counting down; they slowed a bit and finally came to rest with 2011 across the screen. Again the text scrolled on.

When the opportunity for time travel arrives, your phone will start to vibrate and will do so (intermittently) for two hours; after that the time gate will have closed. Don't worry if it is impossible for you to respond right away; you will get another chance later on. If you can go, key 10812 into your phone and then press the black button. We will then tell you as much as we know about your destination and the date of your arrival. Please read all the instructions very, very carefully and memorise what you are told. This will stop you seeming strange or different in your new time period.

Time gate! Wicked! But all that about reading instructions, and memorising – it sounded difficult – like an exam.

When you are ready to leave, make sure you are not overlooked by anyone. TAKE OFF MOST OF YOUR CLOTHES (they inhibit time travel). You may put on a garment like the swimming costume you wore at the pool. Then press the time/space travel disc onto your skin, or, if you are wearing it, onto your swimming costume. You will find that it sticks quite painlessly to your skin. Then press the green button.

How was she supposed to strip off here, there or anywhere? What if she was at school?

On arrival, take the silver disc from the bag and press it on to your forehead. A thin film will came away and seemingly dissolve into your skin. Put the silver backing disc into the bag. Also put the mobile into the bag. This is VERY important. It prevents your mobile from being lost, and so you will always be able to return. You will find appropriate clothes your size waiting for you at your landing site.

If you can, you may help the people you meet, but most of all watch, listen learn; we need information.

When it is time for you to return, the phone will vibrate. Take off your clothes key in 10812 and press the red button. If you are in any danger before then, you can press 10812 and then the red button before the vibrations start. We will be able to transport you back even if you haven't been able to take off the clothes you are wearing. BUT this must only be done if you are facing terrible danger. It can be problematic and uses a great deal of energy.

Hmm, Sarah thought. So there could be some terrible dangers – having her head chopped off, perhaps, like one of Henry the Eighth's wives?

When you get back you will find that, although you seem to have been away for some length of time, in actual fact it has only been a few minutes in your present time. We will contact you via this phone or your computer for a de-briefing exercise, although all you have experienced will have been relayed to us via the camera in the film on your forehead.

The blue light faded, the screen shrank in size and fitted neatly back onto the front of her mobile. Sarah realised that Gonk was still sitting quietly in the centre of the rapidly darkening lawn and that the light from the sitting-room windows spilled out across the grass. All was normal, except that she had been invited to become a time traveller. That was not in the least bit normal.

A time traveller!

Invited because of her ability to spot details and her level of personal courage. Well, they'd got that wrong for a start. Perhaps – oh, what a thought! – perhaps there was another Sarah Lacey living locally, and she'd been chosen by mistake. Sarah suddenly realised that she really wanted to go on the time-travelling expedition. Ideas were already bubbling in her mind.

Robin Hood would be good! Maybe she would be invited to report back on him, or, King Arthur and his Round Table, or St George and the Dragon. She had a theory about that dragon, (she thought it might have been an imported alligator.) Perhaps she should try and contact Anniz and make some sensible suggestions. She certainly did not want to go back to Eyam, the plague village, which they had been learning about in school last year. That would be horrible!

'Sarah, bedtime. What are you doing out there?' called her dad, his head halfway out of the patio doors. Sarah swooped forward, picked up Gonk and bundled him back into his hutch. She had decided that casual, super-normal behaviour from now on was essential. If she was going to be hobnobbing with the likes of St George, Robin Hood, or King Arthur she needed to be relaxed and confident. Robin Hood in Sherwood forest – that would be great

CHAPTER 6

Down the Mine

<u>24 Springbank Drive</u>

As soon as he could, Danny escaped the after-tea-take-an-interest-in-the-children time that his mum and dad thought they should do each evening. He managed to slide off back to his bedroom, despite his mum's quick frown at him for leaving so abruptly, while Jenny was giving a blow-by-blow account of her literacy lesson.

He sent a message off to Kaz at SHARP saying

that he thought he had seen the girl they were looking for on the local television news. Her name was given as Sarah Lacey and she was taking part in a project called 'Swim for You Life,' which had been set up for non-swimmers. Of course, he couldn't be sure it was the right girl but the connection was there with the 'leisure services' clue. He explained that the news item didn't make it clear which particular pool it was, but he would try and find out. Kaz had messaged back his thanks, but nothing else. Then, on Monday evening, when Danny was on his computer, supposedly doing research for his science homework but actually playing an interactive war game with Mark, he was interrupted by a SHARP message.

> Hi Danny, we thought we had got an interception fix on STRAP so that they would not be able to get through to this young girl, but we have now found out that they have some device that gets around our block. We delayed them but we haven't stopped them. We are a trying a new blocking system now – our systems people are working non-stop. We won't know for a day or two your time if we've been successful. If we fail, do you think there is any chance of you being able to contact this girl? Kaz

Danny sent the following message back:

I've been thinking about what I could do. I could try to contact her next Saturday when she is at the swimming pool for the 'Swim for Your Life' session, but I'm not completely sure which pool it is. I've checked the local pools and the 'Swim for Your Life' thing is going on at three. I'm pretty sure I know one pool well enough to cancel that out, so I've got two others to check. I'd have to go there on Saturday morning, quite early. I've already got something set up with my mate Mark, who thinks I'm keen on a girl, and I want to travel the ten-miles-or-so fairly early, without my mum and dad knowing. I sometimes think that being involved with SHARP has turned me into a secret agent.

Danny you **are** a secret agent – and just to reassure you: one of the best. We have two girls now who are shaping up well on their time-travelling exploits, but I don't think either of them could cope with the stuff you're doing.
Keep it up. Kaz.

Danny grinned when he read this. They certainly

know how to keep you on side, he thought. He quickly got back to the game, only to find that Mark had fragged him, and was obviously pretty happy because Danny was nearly always the winner when they played against each other. He sent Mark a quick text to say he had lost concentration because his new girl-friend had got in touch.

Then he started worrying about Sarah Lacey. She looked so young and such a smiley, jolly girl. Suppos-ing STRAP got to her before Saturday? Would she be sent back to somewhere dangerous? Would she get stranded in the past? He couldn't just ring her up and tell her not to go. Besides, he wasn't even a hundred-per-cent sure that this Sarah Lacey was the right girl. It could be a Sarah with another second name beginning with 'L', but somehow he thought not. He was pretty sure the girl he had seen on TV was the right girl. Would she survive, or would she become just another missing child story?

12 Boundary Road

After two days of frustrating inactivity, Sarah was beginning to wonder whether she'd just imagined the whole thing. Then on Tuesday morning in her pocket, she found a strange brown bag, and inside it a small metallic disc with a film surface on one side.

She was walking home from school without Agna (who had music on Tuesdays) and she had just reached the point where they took the short cut along a path that ran through small fields and allotments when her phone started a jarring buzz. To answer it there-and-then was tempting, but she was on a public path and anyone could suddenly appear in front of or behind her. Then she thought of the small space between the bushes where she and Agna used to slip through when they wanted to get into the abandoned orchard running along one side of the pathway. Her feet took over; on their own they walked her through the gap and into the straggling undergrowth around the old neglected trees.

She lent her back against the crumbling bark of one of them and dragged out the phone. The screen shone a fantastic, brilliant blue. *Here goes,* she thought, and tapped in 10812. Black button? Yes or no? Sarah looked at the soft blue sky splattered by the leaves of the apple tree; perhaps in a few seconds time she would come face-to-face with King Arthur himself! Taking a huge deep breath she pressed the black button. The screen on her mobile flashed electric blue and the words spun into focus:

Here we go, Sarah. You will have a great time, I'm sure.
Anniz

For some strange reason, Sarah felt a sudden shiver – not panic as much as fear What if things went wrong? Would she remember everything she had been told? What if she got stuck, frozen into the past? What if … but her last 'what if' went no further, as the instructions started to flash up:

‹Time Zone›
1838

‹Place›
Europe. England. Yorkshire.

‹Landing›
Small village of Silkstone

‹Instructions›
Put on time appropriate clothing. Join the crowd moving up hill

‹Destination›

Pit-brow, Moorend entrance to Silkstone Colliery

‹Conditions›

Heavy rain forecast. Industry buoyant

‹Equipment›

Mobile phone, time/space bag containing silver metallic disc

‹Remember›

›Take off most of your clothes

›Press the time/space travel bag onto bare skin

›Press the green button

›When you arrive, press the disc with the film on it to your forehead

›Put the metal backing from the disc into the bag.

›And most important, put your mobile into the bag!!! You won't get back without it

Remember there will be some clothes nearby for you to put on and remember the previous instructions given to you.

Good luck. I'm depending on you. Anniz.

1838, at the pit-brow of Silkstone colliery? That didn't sound like the correct date or place for Robin Hood or King Arthur, and certainly not Saint George, thought Sarah. She would have loved to have sorted out that question about the dragon. Sarah took a quick glance around the deserted orchard. The hogweed and the bramble fronds reached almost shoulder high. Could she strip off, right down to her vest and pants? Of Course she could: seconds later, in pink frilly knickers decorated with tiny rosebuds, she stuck the strange time/space travel bag onto her tummy where it stuck to her skin tightly, although she could not feel a thing. Then she put her finger on the green button, gulped hard and pressed. A high-pitched whine started immediately. It got louder and louder, as if coming closer, and then ... Nothing.

Grey, chilly morning air struck her skin. She shivered. It looked as if it were dawn. Her bare feet were already wet with dew, and beside them was a neatly folded pile of dirty rags and nothing else. She was standing beside what looked like a much-used path running between small stone cottages – almost a little village – and there she was wearing nothing but her pink pants!

Could those rags really be her clothes?

On examination, she discovered a black, mud-streaked, badly worn pair of canvas trousers, and an equally dirty and torn cotton shirt, and that was all. No shoes. Using the tips of her fingers to hold the garments and with her mouth held shut in a tight, sharp line, she struggled into them. They smelt ghastly, a mixture of soot and toilets. The trousers had no buttons or a zip, just a drawstring round the waist to hold them up.

Oh no! She'd forgotten to put her mobile into the bag, and what about attaching that metallic disc thing to her forehead? She slipped it out and followed the instructions.

All done. Now what? So far, time travel had been cold, wet, and dirty, not entirely what she had imagined. What next?

'Sam, Billy! Come on now, lads, we're late, get a move on.' Sarah spun round; further down the path she could see a man standing in the doorway of one of the cottages. Two small boys tumbled out of the door behind him. They were dressed in the same sort of clothes as she was wearing. The three turned and started walking down towards her.

''Ey up, lass,' said the man as he reached her. ' Not seen you before, who be ye?'

'Sarah…' Sarah stuttered.

'Oh, Ellen Jukes's lass. Heard she was real sick, poor soul. Spitting blood?'

Sarah nodded, at a loss as to what any of this was all about.

'Look, ye come along with us today,' he continued, striding off down the path with the three children tagging along behind. 'My Mary's off poorly and I could do with one more. Sam – she can take over from ye. She'll be the trapper. Billy, ye can hurry, and Sam can thrust. We'll be a real team.' All this was shouted over one shoulder as they scampered along.

The two boys – Sam and Billy, she presumed – shot quick glances at her but said nothing.

The houses soon petered out and now they were trudging up hill on a track between fields with a big wood higher up the hillside. In front and behind them there were small groups of people all walking in the same direction. And way up above them on the skyline was a great sprawling mass of buildings. Sarah could see a huge, tall, thin chimney spitting out a plume of black smoke that smudged the dawn sky. There was a metal wheel clanking round and round and wagons like black rhinos spilling out in all directions. In the distance, she could hear a dull, rumbling sound.

'Not seen ye down t'mine before,' one of the boys finally spoke. Sarah's heart missed a beat.

Mine! She was expected to be going down a mine with them. Of course that's what that colliery word had meant. It was a coalmine.

CHAPTER 7

Don't Mind the Rats

'Tha dad used to be a getter next to our dad before he got sick,' said the older boy, breathing hard as they were almost running to keep up with the long strides the father was taking.

'No, well... I...' Sarah spluttered. What was a getter?

'Now tha mum's poorly, suppose ye do the cooking and all that for her,' he carried on; they seemed to know all about her. While they were thin, with very white skin and strange, almost bald heads, they seemed quite friendly.

'Our sister, Mary, got her hand caught in the winding gear; she's thirteen and does all the hurrying. Me and Sam, we take turns to do the thrusting, and when we not be thrusting we trap. So if ye sit by the trap door, we can manage the corve.'

So, thought Sarah, that one, the talker, the bigger one, he must be Billy, and the smaller one must be Sam.

Hurrying, thrusting, trapper, corve, getter! Sarah

hadn't the faintest idea what they were talking about; she would need every bit of her detecting skills if she were to get on top of all of this.

So far, Billy had done all the talking; Sam had just grinned a cheeky grin.

'How long have you been going down the mine with your Dad?' she asked Sam, smiling. He looked about seven years old to her. He grinned even wider.

'Two whole years, now. Went down first when I was eight. Spent most of the time as a trapper, but now I'm ten and really big, Dad lets me thrust for Mary.' He kicked a few stones with his hard, bare toes and did a sort of little hop. He looked much too small and thin to be ten years old. She was so much bigger than he was.

'Trapper?' dare she show her ignorance?

'Yeah, course. We all start with that. Sit by the trap door and open it when the corve comes up, and close it when it's through. Easy. Have ye got tha candle?' He shot a quick glance towards her hands. Sarah was suddenly conscious that she had red varnish on her fingernails (she and Agna had tried out different colours last night.)

By now they had reached the mine.

Oh, why had she agreed with Anniz? Why did she think it would be Robin Hood or King Arthur? She knew enough of some of the horrible things that had happened in the past. She could have been sent to the plague village, or to one of those huge woollen factories where the owners actually bought children and then, because they were so small, set them scurrying to and fro under the huge, machines.

The buildings they had reached were huge. In front of them, were a massive belching chimney, a tall, cone-shaped tower of metal rods with a clattering wheel high in the air, stone sheds and big railway wagons piled high with coal. A crowd of men streamed over the cobbled yard, and with them there were women and children – some of whom looked no older than seven or eight, and some in their early teens. All were dressed in the same sort of dirty rags as she was.

The big man stopped and looked down at her.

'Tha dad, before he got sick, he was a good mate a mine. We miners have got to stick together. I'd hate to see any of his bairns go hungry. Here.' He unwrapped a piece of cloth and took out a hunk of bread, and broke off a corner. 'Tie that up in tha shirt. Ye not be hurrying, so ye don't need to strip down like the others do. Sam, if ye's thrusting behind the corve ye don't need no candle, so let the lass have yorn. Now don't use it all. That's got to last him all week.'

Sam was no longer grinning, and the look on his face told Sarah he was not at all pleased at having to part with his candle.

Sarah had stopped trying to understand. All she could do was watch, listen, follow and just hope she didn't get any of it wrong.

She took a corner of her tattered shirt, folded it around the hard, dry crust of bread and tied it in place. By now they had walked across the cobbled yard towards a big, stone, open-sided shed.

Billy turned and looked at her.

'Been on a clatch iron before?' Sarah shook her head. She had no idea what he meant.

'To get us all down fast, the men go down in the lift, but Betsy over there with that winch, she lets us little'uns down on the clatch iron.'

The next few minutes were the worst few minutes Sarah had ever experienced. Beside a gaping black hole in the ground stood a woman; down through the hole ran a strong thick rope; and as the women wound up the rope, Sarah saw a round disc attached to it rise up to the surface. In pairs they went. Sarah saw that one child would sit on the disc, while another would leap onto his or her lap and wrap their legs round the body of the first child. Like that, they were lowered into the darkness.

Billy jumped onto the round, swinging disc and nodded to her. Biting the inside of her cheeks and screwing up her face, Sarah stepped out over the gaping hole and dropped down onto his lap, and away they fell, the rope screaming over the cogs of the pulley. The ghastly contraption fell like a stone into the warm, airless depths of the earth.

Thump! They reached the bottom.

'That was so horrible, I could scream,' Sarah declared.

Billy laughed, 'I felt just the same first time I came down, I thought my stomach was going to come right up through my mouth, but ye get used to it. And ye know what? It's the best bit of the day, that is.'

Seconds later Sam banged down behind them; grinning widely.

They were in a huge, warm, lamp-lit cavern carved out of the earth. The rocks and soil were held up by wooden beams, and over the beaten ground ran iron railway lines. It was full of men and children, and small wooden trucks rolling away in all directions.

'Billy, get tha belt on,' the big man ordered. Billy grabbed a heavy leather belt and chain from a hook.

'Sam, get that corve over there.' Sam darted

across to where the trucks were standing and started to push one of the trucks down the metal tracks. Their dad, (Sarah had heard one of the men call him Mr Atick) had, slung his pick over his shoulder and set off.

To begin with they marched down a dimly lit tunnel cut through the rock. Gradually the roof of the tunnel became lower as it branched off into smaller and smaller tunnels. They walked upright at the start, but soon they needed to bend over a little; finally they reached a side opening, where Mr Atick went down onto all fours and scrambled in. Sarah watched horrified as Billy threaded a heavy chain between his legs and then attached one end of it to the belt round his waist and the other to the front of the cart, and then on hands and knees he disappeared into the hole in the wall behind his dad, dragging the wagon behind him.

'No light in there, Sarah,' said Sam. 'I push the corve with my head, see, like this because I'm the thruster. Billy out the front, he's the hurrier. It's real hard work for him when the corve's full of coal. Now, you come up behind me and hold on to my heel else wise ye might get lost.' He stopped for a moment and then whispered, 'We lost some lass not long ago, and no one knows where she ended up.' Not waiting for an answer he dropped down, shoved his head up against the back of the cart and was gone.

In blind panic, Sarah fell onto her hands and knees and with desperate horror crawled into the darkness. Time travel was not all it was cracked up to be. In fact, so far time travel had been dreadful.

Unknown to anyone who was down there in the mine that day, the rain which had started as a gentle drizzle had, by about seven that morning, developed into a heavy, continuous, and at times violent thunderstorm.

But all Sarah was worried about was not losing Sam, and indeed after a few frantic crawls she had bumped right into him; then it had been a long, tedious, painful crawl, down, down, deeper into the depths of the rock, with one hand on Sam, her knees scraping the wet rocky floor and her elbows banging first against one side then the other. Finally they had stopped. Sarah could hear a squeak of a door being swung open and then at last a glimmer of light. In the gloom she could see a shallow cave in the rock wall. Billy had stopped the corve.

'This be tha trap door, Sarah; you sit in that space there, keep your feet tucked under 'cos the corve's right heavy and if it runs over tha ankle it breaks all tha bones. When ye hear the rattle and the banging of it coming along the metal tracks, pull this rope to open the door. It'll be me and Sam, and when we've passed through ye let go the rope so that door bangs shut.' Billy suddenly seemed older and more responsible than before, not really childlike at all.

'Right,' said Sarah, doubtfully. She couldn't see why the silly door was not just kept open.

Billy, as if reading her mind, said, 'If the doors are left open, the good air doesn't go round the mine to where the men are working and the bad air builds up and we all suffocate, or, worse, the damp-fire explodes and we all burn to death.' He paused for a second and then said, almost dismissively, 'And don't mind the rats, they do thee no harm.' And with that he, his brother and the cart rattled off through the door which banged shut behind them, keeping out the dim light that lit the tunnel beyond.

Rats! No one had warned her that time travel would involve rats; or sitting in the dark; or going down a mine – a wet, stinking mine in the dark where she was utterly alone. Alone, wet, in blackness blacker than she had ever experienced, it seemed to press down on her, to crawl into her ears and lungs. Wet blackness you would find in a black cat's mouth. It was hot, heavy, dank air, and there was no way she was going to move an inch from her tiny cave; if she did, she might well get lost, and if she didn't open and close the doors properly the rest might suffocate or get caught in an explosion.

Ages and ages after the boys had first crawled away she heard the bang and rattle of something rolling down the tracks towards her door.

Now she had to pull on the rope.

'How do, Sarah?' She felt rather than saw Billy crawl past her; she heard the clang of the chain between his legs attached to the wagon.

'You OK?'Now it was Sam brushing past her. 'See you soon, we'll be back in no time.' And they were gone and the loneliness swallowed her up again. The one comfort was the fact that it was not cold; in fact, it was a sort of hot, airless, smelly warmth. She knew why it was smelly: Sam had told her to be careful where she put her hands and feet because down the mine there were no privies. It had taken her a bit of time to realise he meant toilets.

When the rat came she stopped breathing. She could hear the scratchy patter of its feet, but had no idea how near it was. In her mind's eye she could see its scaly tail, its skinny paws with yellow curved claws, its sharp pointed nose and horrible long teeth. It was scrambling towards her.

'GO AWAY!' The words just burst out of her. There was a moment's silence and then the worst happened. She felt its horrible feet claw over her legs before it disappeared into the silence, leaving her shaking all over. Sarah Lacey, TV star, time traveller, was crying because of a rat.

CHAPTER 8

Drowned

And on the hillside above them the relentless rain drummed down. The ditches filled and the dry streambeds started to gorge and overflow and the water poured over the hillside down towards the mine.

So the morning passed. They had got to the mine at six that morning, and at mid-day all the children, the hurriers, the trappers, and the thrusters, all straggled out of their dark tunnels into the big dim cavern at the foot of the main shaft, where they sat in little huddles eating their bread and sharing mouthfuls of water.

'Why are there rats in a mine?' Sarah asked as soon as she dared.

'There be good pickin's down here, morsels o'bread and t'like,' replied Sam, making quite sure that none of his crumbs fell through his fingers.

'And bodies, when summat dies, they find the rats get there first.' Sarah was not going to ask more along those lines; she'd heard quite enough.

'It be raining real bad out there at t'mine head,' said Billy as he chewed away at his lump of bread. 'That man over there says the engine what pulls the corves up and down – that sometimes gets stuck when it rains – still that's up there, and we're down here, so it can't hurt us, can it?'

'Ye did real well for a new un, Sarah,' continued Sam, his mouth full of crumbs. 'Cos ye's so big and strong ye can be a thruster before long, and then a hurrier. That is, as soon as ye know the pathways all right.'

Sarah stopped chewing and stared at him. Would she be left down here that long? Would she be expected to crawl on her hands and knees, with a belt round her waist and chain between her legs, hauling a great cart full of coal, straining and dragging it uphill in the total blackness?

'I don't really want to do all that,' she mumbled.

'Ye get paid more!' said Lizzie, a taller girl who had sat down next to her. 'Ye get paid; Billy and Sam's dad doesn't have to stop and take the coal to pit bottom – so he keeps cutting the coal and gets more money – and so altogether ye all get enough money to feed everyone: mum, dad, kids and babbie. Work buys us food.'

'If ye don't work you don't eat,' said Sam firmly.

'Back to work, little-uns!' someone shouted, and they all scattered back to their work. As they walked back Sarah asked: 'why do they call ye a hurrier, Billy?'

He stopped walking and looked at her just a little curiously, and Sarah realised that all the children, even the youngest ones, knew the answers to her questions. But he was a remarkably polite boy, and so he explained, 'Ah, tha knows that! It's 'cos they keep saying to us lads who are pulling, 'Hurry up, Hurry up!' It all makes sense: me dad, he's a getter 'cos he gets the coal from the face; I'm the hurrier, I have to hurry it back to the pit shaft; Sam behind me is thrusting away with his head on the back of the trolley, so he's the thruster and ye's opening and closing the trap door, so ye's the trapper.'

So, once more, there she was, all alone, holed up again in the deep, dark, dreary blackness for what seemed like hours. At one point, Mr.Atick came through the trap door with his lamp.

'Ye stay where ye are for now, I'll be back through in a bit, Sarah,' he said over his shoulder.

More time went by. Then, suddenly, she heard it, a shout. At first it was really a faint echo, and then it was coming nearer and nearer.

'Sarah! Sarah! Come on.' It was Billy, calling as

loud as he could.

He was just at the edge of the cavern, holding a lantern calling to her: 'Come on Sarah. Come on! Something's gone wrong. The top engine's broke and there's water pouring down into the mine! We'll all drown if we don't get out quick.'

Drown? How can you drown in a mine? Suddenly she remembered a story she had heard of how a party of pot-holers had gone caving on a bright summer's day which had suddenly turned stormy, and how the rain water had drained down into the cavern they were in and it had been quite impossible for them to escape in time.

She tumbled forward onto her knees, and, half running half crawling, scrabbled through the darkness to the end of the tunnel, following the dim shapes of Billy and Sam waiting for her with lantern at the point where the small tunnel met the larger one.

'Come on lass. Run, run!' Billy grabbed her arm and they ran through the maze of tunnels together, Sam just a little way in front. Soon, an increasing crowd of folk joined them, all running along the tunnels. No one was wasting breath on talk, all pushing forward as fast as they could without tripping or falling.

Sarah was no longer the girl who had been determined not to learn to swim because she hated water; now she was Sam and Billy's friend and, while she was frightened of the water for herself, she was just as anxious for Sam and Billy and all the other ragged, overworked children who slaved, week in week out, down in the darkness. She forgot about the phone strapped to her waist, forgot that she really lived in the twenty-first century, forgot that she could escape from the mine whenever she wanted just by keying in 10812 and pressing the red button.

At last they reached the vast cavern at the base of the main shaft, through which the corves full of coal were normally hoisted one by one to the surface, except that now nothing was going up. Water was pouring down the shaft, splattering everyone below.

'What's up, why isn't anyone getting pulled up?' asked Billy, fear making him brave. A bony man standing in front of them turned round, and looking down said quietly:

'Rain got into the steam engine; it can't work no more. They got to winch everyone up by hand; it'll take two hour or more to get this lot of men to the surface.'

'What about us little'uns?' piped up Sam, his

voice high and pinched.

'They'll get round to you in time, I guess,' he said doubtfully. 'But ye could try and walk up to the day hole.'

Nobody willingly walked up to the surface of the mine because it was a rugged, hard, upward struggle, up an intensely steep incline. Besides, the route to the day hole was tricky. How could you be sure you wouldn't get lost? It was much quicker to use the winch, but now it would take hours to hand-winch everyone up to the pit brow.

Jim, a tall, scraggy boy of about fifteen, turned to Billy and whispered: 'They'll leave us kids to the very last; they'll get all the men out first, you know that. Come on, let's make for the day hole, Huskers Opening, that's the nearest.'

'Jim! It's miles away, well never get there!' protested Billy.

'All right. Ye wait here and drown. Some of the hurriers have gone that way already.' Jim snapped.

'All right, I'll come with ye, but do ye know the way?'

'Course I do, come on, at least we've got a chance if we go that way. I'm not standing here and waiting for the mine to flood.'

Billy turned to Sarah and Sam, 'Come on ye two, we're getting out.'

Within minutes they were joined by a crowd of children, frightened and silent, all aware that they had to fend for themselves. They clambered on in the complete dark with their hands pressing on the side walls, their feet tripping over rocks, holding onto each other, breathing hard, hurrying.

'Keep together, don't straggle behind. Hold onto the little uns. Someone keep a hold of Joey, he's only seven,' Jim called out. 'I've got to count how many roadways we pass before we turn off.'

Somehow the mine now seemed to be full of noise, rumbles, groans, gurgles, and a sort of roaring noise. Most of the time it was completely black; just occasionally a dim light from a fixed lantern revealed another dark opening.

'This way, lads, through this trap door, and then we have only one more door and we'll be climbing upwards out into the fresh air.' Sarah could just about make out Jim' s words. Because she was not used to moving half on her hands and knees, half bent double, she had fallen way behind the other children. She could hear the stones rolling and scattering under their feet, but they were now some way ahead of her.

'Sarah, come up here!'

Sarah spun round. She could see a dim light held out above her head. An arm reached down and grabbed her hair.

'Lizzie?'

'Come on, up here. I think there is a quick way out, cutting off the corner. I'll pull ye up.' Arms reached down towards her, and seconds later she was hauled up into a tiny crevice packed with children.

'This be the slit,' whispered Lizzie. 'We're above the roadway down there. Even if t'water floods, we're a good bit higher, and…'

She got no further because of the snarl and the splash, the gurgle and roar of what sounded like a river in full flood bearing down towards them. And suddenly they were drenched with the splatter of water from the torrent sweeping along the tunnel just below them. A deluge of water, rocks, mud, and filth, travelling faster than a galloping horse, heaved down the tunnel in which Sam and Billy, Joey and Jim and all the other children had been standing just seconds ago.

Already the torrent had half-filled the tunnel and was rising every minute, higher up towards the base of the slit in which Sarah and the others cowered. The ugly wall of mud, water, and stones was unstoppable, and anything in its path would be doomed.

None of the children in the slit said anything. Squeezed together in a giant huddle of arms and legs and bodies they clung to each other. Sarah could hear their fearful, anguished, frightened sobs. She was wet, battered, and petrified.

'What has happened to them? To those other children in the tunnel?' Sarah managed to whisper.

Nobody replied. They stood silent and still, almost like rock themselves, but the water did not come over their feet. After what seemed like ages but was only a few minutes someone from the back of the slit called out:

'Lizzie? How is the water, can ye reach down and feel it?'

All the children hushed for moment, suddenly aware that the flood was no longer roaring past them. It was strangely silent, just the clattering sound of rocks and pebbles rolling down the passageway.

'It's all gone, all the water has gone, I can't feel anything, it must have washed back towards that last trapdoor,' she said. One of the smaller children started to moan.

Sarah bent down to put an arm around her when

she felt the phone at her waist. Of course, she could escape this nightmare! This living nightmare.

In the dark, she fumbled for the phone and pulled it out of the small bag. She explored the keys with her fingers: yes, she would be able to work out where each number was. Carefully, so as not to make mistakes, she felt for 1 and then 0 and next 8, then 1, now 2. She hoped she'd got them right. Now the red button.

Press.

Nothing.

Press again! Still nothing!

Perhaps the system didn't work underground – perhaps it was like mobile-phone signals in the London underground?

With gut-wrenching clarity she realised there was no quick way of escape. She had to get to the surface.

Without really thinking, desperate with panic, Sarah shouted, 'Come on everybody, the water's draining down into the lower bits of the mine; we have got to get out. NOW. Now, before any more washes down on us. COME ON.'

With just a tiny glimmer of light from Lizzie's lamp and each child clinging on to the one in front, they edged towards the end of the slit. The big ones jumped down onto the tunnel-floor first and caught the smaller ones as they clambered down. Then, still holding hands, they scrambled on up the tunnel, their feet bruised and bashed by the rolling rocks and stones until suddenly, there was a tiny pin-prick of light ahead: the surface.

'We've made it,' whispered Lizzie as they struggled out into the grey, battered daylight. 'But where are the others?'

'They must have …' Sarah began to reply, when one of the younger children yelled.

'Mind out! RAT!'

Glancing down Sarah saw that a rat, bedraggled, soaked and extraordinarily skinny, was escaping from the mine by running between her legs

One, two, three rats!

She gave a howl of horror and leapt backwards into the mine entrance, falling over as she did. She caught her shoulder as she fell but, struggling to stand up, was able to drag out the phone. It took her half a second to punch in the numbers: 1-0-8-1-2. Then the red button.

Please, let it work. Please let her go home. Please!!!

She heard the high-pitched whine winging closer and closer, filling her brain with sound and then…Nothing.

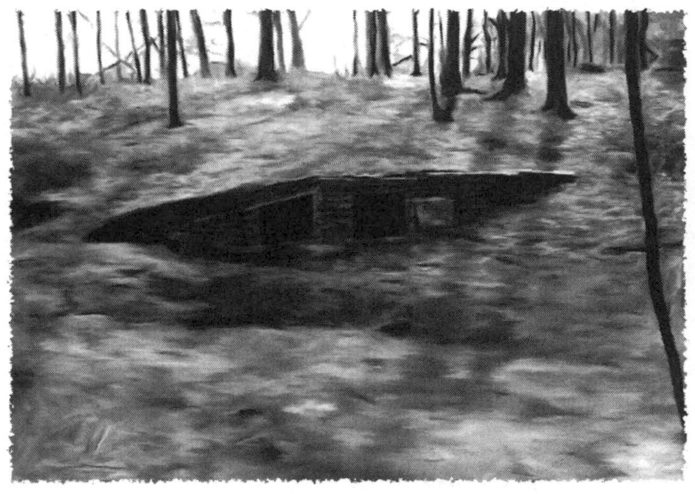

CHAPTER 9

Alton Towers

12 Boundary Road

Sarah opened her eyes, and in front of her were the gently waving leaves of the apple tree. She was blackened with coal dust, streaked with mud, wet from head to foot, with splashes of red blood on her bare feet and hands, but back in the twenty-first century.

Back home!

Then she realised that she was supposed to have taken off her clothes and left them behind. 'Too late now,' she thought, as she stepped out of the torn rags and dropped them on the ground. Her bruised and cut fingers fumbled as she wriggled into her clean, neat school clothes. They felt odd and almost too tight after the looseness of the other ones. As she put on her own clothes, she thought that she would begin to feel like her old self. But she didn't. It was as if the girl she had been down the mine was still with her, standing beside her, almost inside her.

Her mobile buzzed to indicate a text message

and she looked down to see that Agna had sent her a message:

'Gr8 news. Im in the concert at end of term.'

Sarah knew she should text Agna back. That's what Agna would expect. But she couldn't. She just couldn't do it: texting seemed so strange.

She set off walking home as quickly as she could. It was lucky it was Tuesday, the one day of the week when she got home before either her mum or dad. Her head still throbbed and her sight seemed to be wobbly, but she knew she had to get home as soon as possible without anyone seeing her. Then she would have to have a huge wash: her arms, legs, hair, and face were filthy.

24 Springbank Drive

Danny Higgins swerved his bike over to one side of the road. He could feel his phone tingling in his anorak pocket, but there was nowhere safe to get it out because the screen would expand the way it always did with SHARP. He spotted a possibility and rode up behind the carwash – there was a patch of waste ground behind there. Seconds later he was securely entrenched behind a straggly thicket of brambles where he could allow the luminous blue screen to float out from his mobile. The transparent blue sheen hovered mid-air and Danny read:

Kaz here, Danny. We have received some extremely disturbing news. STRAP very nearly lost the Sarah girl. They sent her down a mine. Is there any way you can contact her earlier than planned? STRAP seems to be extremely interested in mining activity, and we're worried that they might try and send her underground again.

'Kaz, I'll try and see if I can track down all the Laceys round about here.

Then I could ring each one up and say I've found a …oh I haven't thought what yet …a something with the name Sarah Lacey on it and ask if they would like me to return it to them.'

Danny spoke as quietly as he could, and then the reply flashed onto the blue screen:

Yes, that seems a good idea. If you contact her, introduce the numbers 10812 to show her that you know what is happening. 10812 is the number STRAP used for this girl. And listen, she needs to be told that time travel is seriously addictive. Good Luck. Kaz.

Danny swung his bike out on to the main road. It was going to be really tricky tracking down this Sarah Lacey kid. He could try the phone book, but some people only used mobile phones these days. He would have to keep his fingers crossed that the Laceys were a bit old-fashioned and still had a landline.

12 Boundary Road

'Hi Mum.' With her wet hair plastered to her head, her arms and legs pink with scrubbing, and her scratched, bruised toes hidden inside socks, Sarah sidled into the kitchen.

'Did I hear the shower?' asked her mum casually. Sarah never, never, never had a shower voluntarily, and certainly not at four in the afternoon.

'I fell off my bike and got really messy.' Sarah tried this out as an explanation, watching her mother's face to see if it was accepted as a reasonable explanation for her taking the much-feared shower; while she herself realised for the first time that the warm, clean water, the perfumed shower gel, and the white towels felt wonderful.

Dad put down his coffee cup and grinned: his daughter was growing up. He'd always believed she'd just naturally get over her water phobia. Perhaps the swimming lessons were having an effect on her after all.

'Did you hurt yourself, Sarah?' he asked. 'I can see a nasty graze on that knee. Are you OK?'

'I'm fine, Dad,' Sarah replied, and then, as he still looked at her with a question in his eyes, she added: 'honestly'.

'Well, I've got a real surprise for you all.'

Her mother put down the knife she was using to cut up vegetables and turned to look at her husband. Sarah did her best to look interested.

'You remember that poem I wrote last time we went to Alton Towers? Well, it won a prize, and this Thursday we have free entrance tickets for the whole family,' he declared, proudly.

Her mum clapped her hands. 'Bravo for the family poet!'

'Well done, Dad.' Sarah tried to sound enthusiastic, but it was a struggle. Her mind was still full of the things she had just seen: children blackened by coal dust, pulling those terrible trucks, alone in the dark. Children dying.

'I've got this school project. Can I use the computer? We're doing this thing on children down the coal mines.'

'Of course, you can, Sarah,' said her dad. 'But I've got a book somewhere on that, got it months ago from Oxfam. *Children of the Dark* it's called; like to have a look?'

Later, Sarah sat on her bed. By now she had read three whole chapters of the book, and had a list in front of her of the children who had been buried in Silkstone Church graveyard. It gave the names of twenty-six children – the oldest, seventeen – the youngest, seven.

They had all drowned; washed back by the torrent of water against the last door they had just passed through. All twenty-six crushed together in a tangle of arms and legs. There were the names of Billy and Sam, Joey, and Jim, and all the others whose names she had never learned.

And there was another name.

Sarah Jukes! That other Sarah had been at the mine after all on that day. The Sarah that Billy's dad had mistaken her for. Sarah whose dad was dead and whose mum was sick. The mother now had no daughter. She was drowned. Sarah tried not to think about it, but it was impossible not to, it took over all of her thoughts.

That night in bed her phone had started that special buzzing. Like an automaton, she had pressed the black button.

Hello Sarah, This is Anniz, We were extremely pleased with your skills in observation. We are sorry that you were precipitated into an unfortunate event. However we now know very much more about the barbaric practices of industry in the nineteenth century.

There was quite a long pause and Sarah said slowly:

'Well I'm not going again, that's for sure.'

STRAP only chooses participants who can cope with all situations because of their ability to use their own initiative.

'If you think that makes me feel any better, you are wrong,' Sarah snapped at the mobile, thumping red, black, and green buttons all at the same time, and stuffing the phone into the very bottom of the dirty laundry bag.

But the events of her visit to Silkstone Colliery filled her mind for the rest of the week.

'Sarah, are you OK?' Agna had asked.

'Sarah Lacey, stop day-dreaming and get on with your work,' her teacher had said, annoyance in her voice.

'I think you are going down with something,' her mother had muttered.

'Come on, Sunshine, lets go to the park!' her father had suggested. 'You can have a go on the climbing wall and then we'll all get an early night. It's Alton Towers tomorrow, you know.'

She was a bit livelier at Alton towers. In fact, the sheer scariness of the rides blasted the memories straight out of her mind.That was until her Mum suggested that they went on the log flume.The first part, when the floating logs bobbed along a shallow channel built almost level with the tree tops, was fun, but then the stream dipped down and the boats were washed along into a darkened tunnel, moving faster and faster, with the water splashing up and over them. Then, Sarah started to scream.It was a dreadful, heart-rending, ear-piercing, blood-curdling scream. She screamed and screamed, curled up in a tiny ball at the bottom of the log canoe long after the ride had stopped. While her frantic parents tried to get her to unwind and climb out of the boat, she continued screaming and sobbing until a medical assistant arrived and, with her parents' permission, gave her an injection. Then, limp and tear-stained, she stumbled on shaking legs out of the boat and allowed them to lead her, still sobbing, to the café.

After a cup of hot, sweet tea and a good wipe down with wet-wipes, Sarah heard the kindly medical lady explain to her mum:

'We do get panic attacks like that on some of the other rides. Most people have no idea what brings them on, but we have never had anyone respond to the floating log flume quite like that before.'

Mrs Lacey nodded, her face screwed up with anxiety. She blamed herself for having suggested they go on the flume in the first place.

'Don't worry, Mum,' Sarah said quietly. 'I'm all right now. I've got over it.' She could not explain that the mine experience had come rushing back, nor that she was screaming and crying for her dead friends; that she was screaming with fear for Billy, and Sam, and all the others. She could not explain that she had screamed the whole incident out of her system and that now she just felt sad. Sad, and calm, and about a hundred years old.

CHAPTER 10

Magpie Mine

'Sarah, I think you need an early night.' Her mum had fussed, and hovered, and fussed again all afternoon, even though Sarah herself felt washed clean, and shaken out, completely clear of her cloud of misery. She had already read, earlier in the week, how the publicity about the mine disaster had prompted the government to bring in laws to stop children and women working down the mine, and how those twenty-six deaths had probably saved the lives of countless other children.

'Oh, Mum, I'm all right now; can I go outside and play with Gonk for a bit? It's a great evening. And I need to re-read a couple of chapters from that book we've been doing in class.' Sarah picked up her school bag and went towards the door into the garden.

'All right, have half an hour out there, but no longer. I'll call you in at nine.'

It was a warm, light evening and Gonk was surprisingly energetic for a very timid rabbit, so she wasn't getting much reading done. Then, chasing after him as he hopped between the greenhouse and the old shed, Sarah felt her mobile start to judder.

Bobbing down behind the shed, she dragged it out. The screen rose, blue and shiny, hovered and then climbed a bit higher before the words appeared:

Hello, fellow traveller. This is Anniz. Huge congratulations. Your dispatches fascinated STRAP; you have added so much to our understanding of early rock extraction methods and the appalling social conditions of the working poor. Your first visit was in 1838.This time we want you to go back to 1836. Would you consider visiting another mine?'

No mention of St George, Sarah noticed, or Robin Hood – not even King Arthur – so she punched her one-word reply.

'NO!'

You were chosen, Sarah, because of your great personal courage, your attention to detail and the skill you possess at fitting in with different cultures. At the moment we do not have another time traveller quite like you.

Now they are trying to flatter me, Sarah thought, just so I'll say 'yes'. But despite herself she started to feel tempted. Her pulse was quickening and she felt incredibly pleased that they found her so good at time travelling; maybe it was a special skill she had? Well, if they wanted her so badly, she might as well try a bit of bargaining.

'I'll say yes, if your lot agree to one of my wishes.'

I've tried the dragon request and got nowhere with it.

No, it's not that. I will go back to the mines if you come along to the swimming lesson tomorrow.

For a few seconds the screen wobbled badly, almost falling out of the air, and then it sort of coughed before text again appeared.

Permission granted; although it is very irregular. It's a deal. I'll be there at the pool tomorrow.

Then the screen went an amazing, deep-purple colour before the next headings flashed up:

‹Time zone›

1836

‹Place›

Derbyshire, the white peak lead-mining area

‹Landing›

Small country town

‹Instructions›

Get changed into the boy's clothes and walk to wards the small manor house

‹Destination›

Magpie lead mine

<Identity>

Boy scribe employed by the surveyor. Expected in the next few minutes

Boy scribe!

Boy?

She was going to have to pretend to be a boy? Oh, it was bad enough having to behave as though she knew what was going on; it was quite another thing to have to do it as a boy. This was not on. Sarah quickly tapped in 10812 and pressed the black button firmly. No response, none whatsoever, not even when she did it a couple more times.

'Drat, drat, and drat.' She spat the words out at the gently snuffling rabbit, who seemed to have settled down now to his usual gentle pace. He was nibbling at the grass along the side of the shed. Almost without realising what she was doing, she was wriggling out of her T-shirt, jeans, socks, and trainers. She fished into her school bag and got out the small, flat time/space bag. She peeked inside. Yes the disc with the film backing was in there. She popped the bag shut and clapped it to her tummy where, just as before, it stuck firm.

Green button.

'Here we go again.' She hated mines. She hated

mines almost as much as she had once hated water. The last thought that flashed through her mind was the possibility that there might be rats, even in lead mines. Then her brain was filled with the high-pitched whine coming closer and closer, then…Nothing.

The transfer was so quick and so gentle it took her a moment to realise that she was somewhere else.

The sun was warm on her bare shoulders. Really beautiful bushes laced with a froth of white flowers surrounded her, and between them she could see the broad backs of some sheep and half-grown lambs. There was a faint haze of bluebell blossom under the trees at the edge of the field. The sound of happily buzzing bees and gently calling lambs filled the air. It was warm and light and springtime. It was lovely.

Where was the mine?

Sarah was about to step out of the bushes when she remembered the clothes, the mobile and the disc. 'Get on with it girl… oh no, boy. Get on with it boy,' she chided herself. Minutes later, the film from the disc invisible on her forehead, she was striding, in a boyish fashion, down a wide green path leading to a small cluster of houses. She decided a jaunty whistle would complete her transformation. She'd call herself Sam. Or maybe Simon, or even Sidney!

'Oh, good heavens! They get younger every time! I suppose you do know your letters, boy? And what do they call you? Smart lad though, I must say! How old are you anyway?'

Wearing her new clothes, she had found the manor house with no trouble at all, and was now faced with this big, blustery man who spoke in exclamations and questions.

'I'm Sidney, Sir, and I'm fourteen.' Lying was essential when you were a time traveller. 'And yes, Sir, I know my letters and my numbers.' She hoped that she wasn't lying about this and that the letters and numbers he was referring to were the same as the ones she knew. She agreed with him, though: she did look smart in her grey wool trousers, blue velvet jacket, sparkling white shirt, shiny buckled shoes, and little satchel full of paper, pens, and pencils. She moved slightly to one side as he breathed strong alcoholic fumes all over her. No one looking as good as she did would be actually going DOWN the mine, she thought happily. Oh no.

'Good, good, got your pads I see. Don't call me 'Sir'; I'm Mr Wilson, the best surveyor in the county. Into the carriage! No time to waste! You can manage going down the climbing shafts I presume. No ladders, no winding gear, just one foot on each wooden ledge on either side of the shaft. No fooling around! It's a long way down, 300 feet, I believe.' He strode past her, leaving a small cloud of alcoholic haze as he climbed up into the beautiful little horse-drawn carriage standing on the smooth gravelled drive in front of the stone house.

'In you get, lad, no time to waste! Off we go, Ephraim,' he ordered the driver. They bowled along in silence for a while, Sarah enjoying listening to the clip clop of the horses' hooves. Then Mr. Wilson turned to her and said:

'Dreadful business! Dreadful! In my opinion it was murder. Although what the judge thinks is another matter. I mean, if you take straw and pitch down a lead mine, light the straw, and then throw on the pitch, what do you get?' he glared at Sarah.

'Er...' she had no idea. What was pitch? She had seen straw burning in fields after harvest and it made a lot of smoke. 'Smoke?' she suggested.

'Smoke indeed! Black smoke! Sulphurous smoke! Poisonous smoke! You know what pitch is, don't you? It's tar! It is a killer when lit. And if you set the fire going in the entrance to the one-and-only tunnel leading away from the workings, with men at work further in, what do you get?'

'Trouble.' Sarah thought of the trap doors carefully controlling the flow of air around the coalmine. She was extremely confused. 'Why would anyone want to do that?' she asked, horrified, as they trotted up the steep wooded valley leading away from the town.

'You ask me? You ask *them*, the Magpie mine men! You ask them! They must have been the ones who did it, because it was the Red Soil men who got trapped and suffocated. All three of them; all fathers, all husbands.' He was silent for a bit as they entered a small village. 'I can understand the Red Soil widows putting a curse on the mine. Not that I believe in cursing myself, still.' At that point he turned and tapped the driver on the shoulder. 'Stop here, Ephraim; time for a quick draught, I think.' They stopped outside a small, stone-built pub.

'Won't be long, lad. Go for a walk or something.'

Sarah climbed out of the carriage with her mind in turmoil. Murder, curses. Magpie mine, Red Soil mine. Whatever was all this about? As Mr Wilson was entering the pub, she ran after him.

'Excuse me, Sir, but are we going DOWN this mine?'

He paused, and was suddenly serious.

'We are going down the Magpie lead mine. I am a surveyor; I will work out which lead seam belongs to the Magpie mine and which seam of lead-bearing rock belongs to the Red Soil mine. Deep underground the rock seams criss-cross each other, and so nobody can work out which lead-bearing seam belongs to whom. When I've got a good working map, we can tell each group of miners where they can and cannot dig, and perhaps there will be no more murders and no more cursing. I hope so. I'll measure, you write down my figures. Right?'

Sarah nodded, with the words: 'no more murders, no more cursing' fixing themselves in her mind.

The village they had stopped at would have been thought of as charming in the twenty-first century. There were small, solid, grey-stone cottages, many with little front gardens full of flowers, a farmhouse, and small, open-fronted shops. A few big chestnut trees stood at one end, and the green hills rolled away into the distance. Sarah explored it all, and finally, as Mr Wilson had still not come out of the pub, she wandered down a long, narrow pathway between two cottages leading out to a wide grassy field.

She had bobbed down to re-buckle one of her

smart, shiny black shoes when she heard two men talking quietly on the other side of a stone wall.

'Bert, look at you! Tuck that stuff in tighter.'

'It scratches.'

'Of course it scratches. Straw scratches, man, but they'll see it if you leave wisps trailing below your jacket. Can you see where I've got the pitch?'

'No.'

'Well, just let me say there's no bread in my lunch tin. Just let me say it will need a good scrub out before I put bread back in there.'

'Good idea, that! In your snack tin! If we smoke out that other lot once and for all, then that seam of rock is ours for good.' The men were beginning to walk on ahead of her. So, still bent double, Sarah crept along level with the two speakers, and heard something which made her blood stand still.

'Some bigwig be going down there today, we just might cook his goose as well.' Then their conversation became indistinct as they turned away from the wall.

She stood up slowly, and slowly repeated the conversation in her mind just to make sure she had remembered it correctly. She had heard two words quite clearly: 'straw and PITCH.' She knew what Mr Wilson had told her. He had said that straw and pitch burn to make poisonous, black smoke.

No more murder, no more curses! That seemed unlikely now. After what she had heard today there might be both, and if she climbed down the mineshaft with Mr Wilson, they both might experience the poisonous smoke, and this time there would be no Billy and Sam to show her how to escape.

CHAPTER 12

Straw and Pitch

Sarah ran back to the village as fast as she could, but even so it took her several minutes. She was gasping for breath as she got near to Mr Wilson's carriage just as Mr Wilson, supported by Ephraim, staggered out of the pub. He attempted to put one foot on the carriage step to pull himself up, but the effort proved a little too much.

'Mr Wilson! Mr Wilson, there is going to be another attack on...' the words were tumbling out of Sarah's mouth. Mr Wilson turned to look at her and then held up a hand to stop her.

'Quiet lad, Quiet! No shouting, no talking, no nothing! Just a little nap, I think. Ephraim. Up we get! Down we sit! Off we go! Sleep! Good idea! Yes, lad, sleep is a very good idea.'

Somehow the driver managed to bundle Mr Wilson up the steps and into the carriage. Once seated, Mr Wilson slumped back into a profound slumber. Sarah scrambled up behind him. What should she do now? She turned and tugged on the driver's sleeve. The driver, now eager to get off, had shaken the reins, and the horses had pricked up their ears. Sarah, realising that she could get no sense out of Mr. Wilson, sat down beside the driver.

'Ephraim. There's going to be another fire. I know it. We have got to warn the miners. Warn them all to get out, both the Magpie miners and the Red Soil men because I don't know which side those men were on.'

The driver, keeping his eyes on the road, said quietly – so as not to disturb Mr Wilson, Sarah presumed:

'And how do you know all this, then young man?'

As quickly and quietly as she could, Sarah recounted all she had heard.

'And you have no idea if it were the Red Soil men or the Magpie workers you overheard?' was the first question he asked when she had finished the story.

'No, I don't know the men from around these parts.' That seemed a reasonable answer.

'Good. Just you leave it to me, laddie. I'll make sure everyone knows what's afoot. We will get all the men out of both mines as soon as possible. Look! There's Magpie already; Red Soil is a bit further on.'

They had rounded a bend in the road, and there, across the hillside, stood a tall stone tower, a cluster of buildings, and the huge, horse-driven winding-wheel of the mine. Men were scurrying about, and piles of broken rock where dotted about the place in untidy heaps. After a few minutes, the driver pulled up next to a small outhouse.

'We need the horn. Sidney, can you just slip into that shed there and get it for me? You'll find it hanging on the wall.'

Pleased to be doing something, Sarah jumped down and ran to the shed. She wondered if the sounding of the horn signalled to the men to leave the mine. It was very dark in the shed, and it took quite some time for her eyes to accustom themselves to the lack of light. There didn't seem to be a horn anywhere. Suddenly, the little light there was disappeared, and Sarah spun round as the door behind her swung shut and she heard a heavy clunk. She stumbled across to the door and pushed. It didn't move. She pushed harder and harder, and then tried twisting the handle. She fumbled around trying to find a latch or other means to open the door. Then she began to bang her fists on the door, shouting and yelling. Slowly she realised what had happened. She had been locked in.

Why? Who would have done such a stupid thing? Feeling a horrible sense of frustration she turned round and lent her back against the door, slowly sinking down until she was sitting on her heels, her head in her hands. She had been so keen to get to the mine so that she could warn everyone of the dangers. Right now, at this very moment perhaps, a lit match was being held against a bundle of straw. Perhaps they were just waiting for it to catch fire before throwing over the pitch, which would smoulder into the poisonous, choking fumes.

Gradually it came to her that it must have been the driver, that Ephraim fellow, who had tricked her; perhaps he had known already what was going on. Maybe he had got Mr Wilson drunk so that he could not go down the mine; maybe he was on the same side as the men whom she had overheard – whichever side that was.

After a while she realised that the shed was not completely dark. Dappled light filtered through the cracks between the tiles on the roof. And in the dim light she could see the place was almost empty. The floor was made of rough stones, the walls the same, and there was one heavily boarded window. It was a prison.

A sudden movement came from the darkness of one corner where there seemed to be a pile of sacks. It sent a shudder through her. Rats! There must be rats in there. She was locked inside a prison with a rat! Sarah found that she was shivering; fear gnawed at her with sharp rat teeth. Then she heard another sound.

'Meow, meow,' came quite loud and clear, followed by other much smaller, squeakier meows. And out of the gloom, on dainty white feet, came a small, smudgy cat; smudgy because its coat was black, ginger, grey, and white in an untidy mix. And tumbling behind it, round and chubby, three puff-ball kittens. All four seemed anxious to make friends.

'Hello, little lovely!' cooed Sarah, holding out a finger.

The mother cat came forward, already purring, and for the next few minutes, Sarah forgot she was in a prison and all her worry about mines and burning straw as the kittens clambered over her and the smudgy cat wound itself round her legs. Without realising it, the unpleasant feeling of hopelessness was being replaced by her usual good sense. She said out loud, as if addressing her new friends:

'Attention to detail, great personal courage and an ability to get on with others, remember that, Sarah

Lacey.'

Attention to detail? Sarah forced herself to look around more closely. She had thought the place empty, but clearly that was not the case. There were a few large boxes of some sort along one wall, and in one corner there was a pile of boards leaning against the wall – some boards taller than the others. The tops of the tallest planks were only a few feet away from the roof tiles.

She wondered if she could try scrambling up them; she had always been good at climbing. She saw that several shorter planks were stacked at one side at an angle. It was a steep angle, but perhaps it wouldn't be too difficult to hold onto the sides and walk or crawl up. She decided that bare feet would be better than wearing the stiff, shiny boots. Unbuckling each boot, and slipping them off, she pulled the straps under her belt so that she could fasten them up again around the belt itself. Ready: now, with hands and feet exploring, she cautiously started to inch her way up the shorter planks. It was not easy. Splinters stuck into her skin and the angle of the boards was really too steep. It was only where one board crossed over another that she was able to wedge her toes between them and pull herself up. But she made headway and realised that she only had a little further to go to get herself to the top.

Oh no! Suddenly, the whole pile slithered back away from the wall. Sarah froze. The boards shifted but remained upright. With one hand outstretched she reached up and grasped the top edge of the stone wall.

Done it! She had clambered to the top of boards, and from there it was almost easy to feel the roof above her. There were the tiles. The first one she touched felt quite loose. She pushed hard, and with a resounding clatter a tile tumbled down onto the ground outside. The sunlight streamed through. If she could just lever off about three more she would have a hole big enough for her to climb through.

Hanging on to the top of the wall with one hand and wiggling each tile back and forth with the other, Sarah slowly but surely managed to loosen tile after tile until she had quite a big hole. With a massive effort, she hoisted herself up so that she was sitting on the very top of the stone wall of the shed.

All around lay the wide-open hillside, the grass, the sheep, the tumbled piles of stone and the grumbling clatter of machinery. But there was no one near enough to hear her, if she shouted for help, and anyhow, whom could she trust if she did call?

The drop down to ground level was much too

high for her to jump down. In the park there was a climbing wall, but it was much lower than this. Still, she thought, if you can climb up and down two metres perhaps you can do four. She had climbed up, so now she had to climb down. No one was going to help her. It was up to her.

The wall of the shed was very roughly constructed, so some stones stuck out, while between them were hefty cracks. She turned hand-over-hand so that she was facing the roof, and slowly, cautiously lowered herself over the top edge of the wall.

'Careful, careful,' she said out loud to herself. Testing each crack or cranny between the blocks, she now stretched down as far as she could and began to climb down. Her face was pressed up against the wall, her toes searched for narrow ledges on which to stand and her fingers jammed tight into crevices.

It took an age, but there she was. She jumped down the last four feet and it was as she landed on the soft turf that the heavy hand fell on her shoulder.

'And what's all this about?' Sarah spun round and stared up at the red and puzzled face of a slightly swaying Mr, Wilson.

'Ephraim told me that once we had reached the mine you'd yelled: 'I'm not going down no mine with a curse on it!' and that you'd jumped out of the carriage and run off.'

Perhaps it was her time with the children down the coalmine, perhaps it was because she had been tricked and locked in the shed, but suddenly Sarah was really angry.

'I don't care which side you are on. I don't care if you want the Magpie miners to get the lead or the Red Soil miners. It's bad enough having to be down there every day just to earn enough money to feed the family. It's bad enough to be out of the fresh air and the sunshine, to be in the dark and the stink. Do you realise there are no toilets at all down there?' (Oh, I bet 'toilet' is a modern word, she thought in the middle of her outburst, I should have said 'privy'.) ' But nobody should be in danger of suffocating on top of all that.' She shouted up at him, her face red and angry.

'Wait a minute, young man. What's brought this on? Who says they are going to suffocate?' Mr Wilson spluttered, taking a step back. And so once more Sarah recounted the overheard conversation, and this time the reaction she got was totally different.

'Come on, Sidney, no time to waste! We've got to run, over there into that shed! Quick!'

Within seconds Mr Wilson had shouted the story

into the concerned face of the mine foreman, who immediately sent two messengers, riding bareback on the packhorses, across the field to the mine head of Red Soil.

Before long the whole place seemed like a giant ant hill, with men and boys popping out of holes in the ground here there and everywhere, and with an amazingly sober Mr Wilson shouting at everyone.

Suddenly a shout rang out across the stony hillside:

'Look, Sir. Look what be found! ' There was an angry buzz from some of the men clustered round the agent's office as a pile of bone-dry straw and a jar of thick black pitch was dumped in the doorway.

'So, where was this lot found?' bellowed Mr Wilson.

'No way to tell, Sir. That bit down there could be Red Soil working, but then again it might be Magpie diggings,' muttered the man who had stumbled across the incriminating evidence.

The foreman glanced across to Mr Wilson and shrugged, as if to say: 'You see the difficulty!'

'This is not my business!' Mr Wilson said coldly. 'You deal with it! A crime has been committed in the past, and it looks as though someone was planning to repeat it. So make sure you question every man who is left up here, even though no doubt all the guilty ones will have slipped off home already.' Mr Wilson turned to march out of the shed. 'But I'm taking this lad back down to town and I need to have a very serious word with my driver.'

Grabbing Sarah, he said, 'Come lad, I'll not have you questioned, as you did not see the two culprits and you did raise the alarm as soon as you could.' A sharp, crisp wind blew across the rocky hilltop as they made their way back to where the carriage and pony had been secured.

'I knew that story Ephraim had spun was non-sense, you'd left your satchel in the carriage, and no scribe leaves the tools of his trade behind,' said a surprisingly agile Mr Wilson as he hopped up onto the carriage and gathered up the reins. 'In you get, son.'

'Certainly, Sir, but can we please let the cat out of the locked shed before we go?'

They went back to the shed and pulled back the heavy iron bolt, leaving the door ajar for the cat. Then they got back in the carriage and trotted away down the country lane between the pink and white elder-berry blossom and the billowing shepherds parsley. Mr Wilson turned to Sarah and, with a huge wink, said:

'Now then, when we get back, Sidney, not a word to the dear wife about the brief stop at the hostelry. Lovely lady! But she's taken the pledge and not a drop of liquor passes her lips. You'll stay with us for a bite of supper – rabbit pie I believe, followed by junket. What?'

Sarah was surprisingly hungry, but rabbit? She was not sure about that; Gonk was at this very moment hopping around the garden.

'Rabbit pie?' she said, uncertainly.

'Shot them myself,' said Mr Wilson, proudly. 'I can tell you, if we don't eat the rabbits they'll eat us, or rather our carrots, our peas, our cabbage, our lettuce. I had an entire row of early peas eaten to ground level this year by those varmints.' The carriage was bouncing down the narrow lane running down the length of the dale, high stone walls on each side with the sweet, musty smell of elderflower filling the air. It seemed impossible to believe that underneath the road were the twisted mine works, with their tangled tunnels and snaking drainage channels.

Sarah stayed for supper, and the rabbit pie was delicious, and the homemade ginger beer strong, although she wasn't at all sure about the junket stuff. In the gathering dusk she waved goodbye to the small, plump Mrs Wilson and the big, round-bellied Mr Wilson and managed to walk on about a hundred yards down the road and round a bend into a field before dragging off her clothes, pressing 10812 on the mobile and then, slowly and rather sadly, the red button.

Again that soft whine growing higher and stronger as it enveloped her and then…Nothing.

Between drawing in one mouthful of air and puffing it out again she was transported from then to now. Gonk was still wiffling as he hopped slowly towards her, and her mother's voice was echoing through the evening gloom.

'Sarah, I'm sorry – it's gone nine o'clock, bedtime. Do you want some supper, choc-chip ice cream, before you go up?'

Quick! Clothes! she thought. Whatever would her mum think if she actually came out into the garden and saw her standing there in her pants? Jeans, T-shirt and trainers, quick!

'Mum? I thought junk food was a modern sort of thing?' she said, as she sidled, a little untidily, round the back door. 'What was that junket stuff they used to eat?'

'Good heavens! They are going into details at

school. My granny made junket. You get fresh milk and add rennet, that's a liquid from a calf's stomach.'

'What?' Sarah exclaimed. She paused. The spoonful of choc-chip ice cream was half way to her mouth. She had been eating stuff made with liquid from a calf's stomach – there are some unexpected hazards in time travel!

CHAPTER 13

Where Is Anniz?

Sarah wondered what the clever people of the future would make of her last report. She had lain in bed awake for half the night thinking about it. Thinking how desperate the men must have been to go to those lengths to ensure that they got out the rock full of lead ore. Was it as hard to dig out as coal? Did the men have to lie on their backs in the dark, chipping away at the rock face? Did the children have to carry the rock to the surface? Did the mines flood? Were they full of explosive gas? All that hard work just to make enough money to get food on the table!

At breakfast next morning she asked: 'Are there any lead mines we can visit?'

'Lead mines? I thought your project was on coalmines? Well, Derbyshire is full of old lead pits; it was a thriving industry once. But really hard work – harder and heavier than coal and the pay was rubbish,' said her dad.

'Really?'

'The mines were forever flooding, and getting

filled with inflammable gas; they were too narrow for pit ponies or carts, and the women and children had to process the ore on the surface, and that produced poisonous dust. It was a hard life.'

'What do people do with all that lead? You don't put much in pencils.'

'That's not proper lead. No, they used to use it for gunshot, and for gutters, and for holding glass in church windows. Now it's used in the batteries that we need all the time, and it used to be found in petrol, paints, and china.'

'Why not now?'

'Because it's poisonous, and always was,' said her mum firmly, picking up her coat and bag. 'See you later.' And she hurried out.

'Wow,' Sarah said. 'All those people slaving away underground for a metal which killed you.'

Her dad looked up from his paper, surprised how thoughtful Sarah was becoming.

'Swimming today. All right about that?'

'Sure,' she grinned. Only a week, only a week ago she had not met Anniz, not been down a coalmine or to a lead mine, not been nearly drowned, and not been involved in fire-raising, and here it was, swimming lesson time again.

'Oh, they found your goggles.'

'Goggles?'

'Yes, the ones you left at the pool last week; this boy who had a class after yours picked them up by mistake and thought they were his. He got our name from the phone book. He said he has a STRAP pair 10812, same as yours.'

Sarah stared at her dad. She didn't have goggles. Mum knew that, but mum had already left. And nobody except herself and Anniz knew about STRAP or the 10812 number.

'What's he going to do with my goggles?' she asked, her mouth strangely dry.

'Said he'd be there at the pool because you'll need them. His name is Danny...um...Danny Higgins. I think.'

Sarah glanced out of the window: the taxi was already waiting for her. Grabbing her swimming bag, she stumbled out of the house. What was going on? Anniz hadn't mentioned Danny to her. And Anniz wasn't in the taxi yet, and when the driver stopped at the museum to see if he was waiting there, he was nowhere to be seen. Nor was he at the pool.

The bossy lady was. It was she who called the register while Bill stood next to her doing painful and slightly silly stretches. Sarah was not just confused, she was disappointed and grumpy as well. She wanted to meet Anniz. He'd made the swimming such fun. Just as the lesson was about to start, Sarah plucked up her courage. She put up her hand and said:

'Excuse me, but the partner I had last week, Anniz – where is he?'

The bossy lady flushed a bright pink. 'Ah yes, well, in fact, actually, it seems, um, of course, sometimes a candidate goes off and, er…' She paused, and then said, snapping the register shut with a quick slap, said: 'He's not here.' And with that she turned and marched off.

'Bill…?' Sarah pleaded. 'What did she mean?'

Bill chortled. 'Nobody knew where that little lad came from, how he got on the list, or which school he attended. He didn't even have a surname.'

The lesson was OK, and Sarah was so determined to learn to swim she got on well but, without Anniz, it was not the same. Still, she was the first to get dressed and walk into the little café. She had just got a biscuit and a drink, when somebody said her name.

'Sarah, Sarah Lacey?'

'That's me,' she replied. Sarah spun round to see a boy, quite a bit older than her, looking at her intently.

'Does 10812 STRAP mean anything to you?' the boy asked

'Yes?' she replied. And then in a rush: 'Do you know where Anniz is?'

'Anniz? Is he your contact at STRAP?'

Sarah nodded.

'Look, I'm Danny Higgins, a time traveller like you, and I've been sent to warn you about the dangers of the STRAP organisation.'

Sarah sat down opposite Danny. It felt unbelievably odd having this conversation.

'You're a time traveller as well?' she asked, as if she were asking if he played football.

'Yes, I am. I know it's a strange thing for us to be talking about. But, Sarah, you are really a little too young to be time travelling.' Danny could see that this remark had annoyed his new acquaintance, so he added:

'That sounds a bit patronising of me, but I can assure you there are good medical reasons why that is so. And, as I've just said, I've come to warn you about the dangers with STRAP.'

'Dangers? Well, I know I almost drowned and then I was nearly involved in a fire, but that wasn't their fault.' Sarah took a large bite of chocolate biscuit.

They were sitting at a small table facing out onto the pavement, which was helpful as neither of them wanted other people to hear what they were saying. In a few quick sentences Danny explained about the organisation called SHARP – people from the future who had contacted him – and told how they had been infiltrated by an organisation called STRAP, which seemed to have no qualms about putting the children they sent back in time into dangerous situations.

'STRAP work fast and without any safety regulations and stuff like that,' said Danny. 'I've been trying to figure out for some time whether I can believe all that is told to me by these people supposedly from the future. I mean, for all I know they could be some kind of aliens. The one thing I do know is that SHARP's systems all seem much more reliable than those of STRAP's.' Danny was silent for a moment, then he said, more slowly and quietly:

'They have told me that what they are doing with our help is preventing the future destruction of the earth. To tell you the truth, I don't really know about this, but I do know that we time travellers must look out for each other. And right now my job is to warn you not to go with STRAP.'

'But Anniz was so nice, and even if it was scary I

sort of wanted to go back a second time, and ...' Sarah began to feel a little scared, realising what risks she had taken.

'Did they tell you that you might become addicted to time travel? Or that it might have a deleterious affect on your health? Did they promise to get you out no matter how dangerous things got? Did they give you time to think it all through before agreeing?'

Sarah looked at him in surprise; she had not considered any of this.

'Did SHARP tell you all of that?'

'Well, I did not take it all in to begin with, but yes. I think as things are going at the moment there will be some serious conflict between the SHARP people and the STRAP bunch before long.'

Sarah looked at Danny carefully; he seemed very young to be talking about such grown-up things, 'I don't think I want to get caught up in anything as tricky as all of that,' she said firmly. Danny smiled. He looked much younger when he smiled.

'If those STRAP people get in touch again, will you contact me?' He scribbled his mobile number down on a piece of paper. 'Keep this number safe. Oh, and by the way, you've been awarded this BAFTA.'

'Bafta? I thought film stars got those.'

'Well, SHARP discovered what you'd done when they intercepted the STRAP file on you and they awarded it to you. It's BEST AGENT FOR TERRESTIAL ASSISTANCE It was for the way you encouraged the children to leave the mine and how you warned the owners when the fire-raisers were at work. They told me all about it. You were incredibly brave.'

He slid a tiny medal across the table. It looked as if it was made from some rather dull metal, but when Sarah picked it up she saw colours shifting and changing, shimmering all over its surfaces, which seemed to change shape even as she looked at it.

'That's lovely,' she said.

Back home, her dad was waiting by the gate for Sarah to arrive. He looked really pleased with himself.

'Good news! We've got it, Sarah. We can go round straight away and get started.'

'Got what?'

'An extra strip on the allotment. I'll put in parsnips this year.'

'Oh, Dad, you got me all excited – how can anyone think an allotment is good news?' Parents were weird. 'Why do you want one anyhow? We can buy vegetables and stuff,' she enquired when they sat down in the kitchen. She searched out the biscuit tin. She was starving.

'My granddad had an allotment; his dad had a bit of ground; and his dad had a back garden where he grew enough vegetables to feed the family.' Her father plugged in the kettle. 'My great-great-granddad, now, he would snare rabbits for the pot, and grow the carrots and onions and potatoes to go with it. That's what he did on Sunday.'

Sarah remembered Mrs Wilson and her rabbit pie. Lucky Gonk, to be allowed to live safe and sound in a hutch!

'Why Sunday?' she asked, taking her third biscuit.

'Well, in those days, back in the eighteen eighties, that was the only day the miners had off work,' said her dad, pouring out three cups of tea.

Her mum had been sitting quietly, and then she said. 'Your father's family come from coalminers, and mine were lead miners.'

Sarah felt a huge lump rising in her throat and tears pricking behind her eyes, although she could not for the life of her say why.

'Yes,' she thought, 'and in some ways I am as well. I'm a time traveller, coal miner and almost, lead miner.' Perhaps if she got to go with SHARP, she thought, they'd really let her meet Robin Hood, or King Arthur, and somebody ought to clear up that matter about St George's dragon.

Acknowledgements

The writer gained inspiration and information for this story from the excellent book 'Victoria's Children of the Dark' by Alan Gallop. It describes in detail children's life and death underground in Victorian England.

Competitions And Activities

Seven Arches Publishing often runs competitions for you to enter with prizes of book tokens, that can be spent in any bookshop, for solving puzzles or for a good illustration. Why not go to www.sevenarches-publishing.co.uk and check out whether there is competition or activity on its way based on one or other of our books. We often include the winning entries of our competitions, or the writing, poems or pictures that you send us in the next print run of the title.

Contact Us

You are welcome to contact Seven Arches Publishing by:

Phone: 0161 4257642

Or

Email: admin@sevenarchespublishing.co.uk